# THE LITTLE CATS

# BOOK

# For Samuel, Jack and Henry

**THIS BOOK BELONGS TO**

...................................................................

# THE LITTLE CATS

ABC

## BOOK

# MARTIN LEMAN

**SIMON & SCHUSTER BOOKS FOR YOUNG READERS**
Published by Simon & Schuster
New York · London · Toronto · Sydney · Tokyo · Singapore

**is for ABBIE,
a marmalade
cat.**

**is for BARNEY,
who sat on
a mat.**

 **is for CHESHIRE,
well-known for
his grin.**

 **is for DAISY,
who wouldn't
come in.**

is for ELVIS,
a cat with
white socks.

is for FANNY,
asleep on
a box.

**is for GARY,
who's watching
a bee.**

**is for HARRY,
who climbed
up a tree.**

is for IDA,
who stayed
in the house.

is for JACK,
chasing after
a mouse.

is for **KITTY**,
whose fur feels
like silk.

is for **LEO**,
seen lapping
his milk.

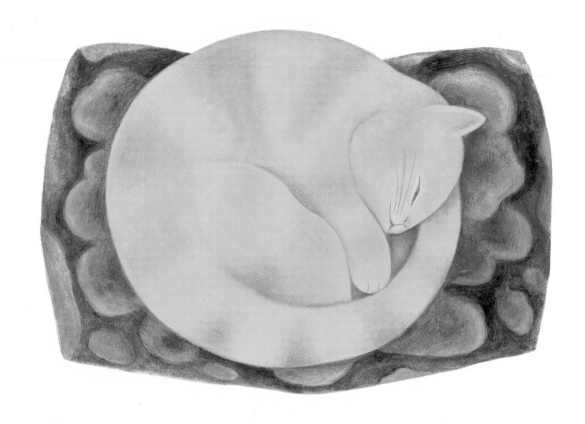

 is for MUFFIN,
curled up in
a ball.

 is for NELLIE,
high up on
a wall.

is for OSCAR, adrift in a dream.

is for PATSY, whose eyes are bright green.

is for QUEENIE,
atop the best
chair.

is for REX—
they make a
great pair.

 is for SIMON,
who stayed out
all night.

 is for TOBY,
in smart black
and white.

is for URI,
who's in quite
a fix.

is for VERA,
who's up to
her tricks.

is for WILLY,
with plenty
to eat.

is for XERXES,
the king of
our street.

is for YOKO,
seen meeting
a friend.

is for ZACH,
and that is
the end.

 **A** is for ABBIE,
a marmalade
cat.

 **B** is for BARNEY,
who sat on
a mat.

 **C** is for CHESHIRE,
well-known for
his grin.

 **D** is for DAISY,
who wouldn't
come in.

 **E** is for ELVIS,
a cat with
white socks.

 **F** is for FANNY,
asleep on
a box.

 **G** is for GARY,
who's watching
a bee.

 **H** is for HARRY,
who climbed
up a tree.

 **I** is for IDA,
who stayed
in the house.

**J** is for JACK,
chasing after
a mouse.

**K** is for KITTY,
whose fur feels
like silk.

**L** is for LEO,
seen lapping
his milk.

**M** is for MUFFIN,
curled up in
a ball.

 **N** is for NELLIE, high up on a wall.

 **O** is for OSCAR, adrift in a dream.

 **P** is for PATSY, whose eyes are bright green.

 **Q** is for QUEENIE, atop the best chair.

 **R** is for REX— they make a great pair.

 **S** is for SIMON, who stayed out all night.

 **T** is for TOBY, in smart black and white.

 **U** is for URI, who's in quite a fix.

 **V** is for VERA, who's up to her tricks.

 **W** is for WILLY, with plenty to eat.

 **X** is for XERXES, the king of our street.

 **Y** is for YOKO, seen meeting a friend.

 **Z** is for ZACH, and that is the end.

SIMON & SCHUSTER BOOKS FOR YOUNG READERS
Simon & Schuster Building, Rockefeller Center
1230 Avenue of the Americas, New York, New York 10020
Copyright © 1993 by Jill and Martin Leman
Originally published in Great Britain by
Victor Gollancz, an imprint of Cassell.
First U.S. edition 1994. All rights reserved
including the right of reproduction in whole
or in part in any form.
SIMON & SCHUSTER BOOKS FOR YOUNG READERS is a trademark
of Simon & Schuster. Manufactured in Belgium

10  9  8  7  6  5  4  3  2  1

*Library of Congress Cataloging-in-Publication Data*
Leman, Martin. The little cats ABC book / Martin Leman.   p.   cm.
Summary: An alphabetical of presentation of twenty-six cats,
from marmalade Abbie to Zach at the end.
[1. Cats—Fiction.   2. Alphabet.   3. Stories in rhyme.]
I. Title.   II. Title: ABC book.   PZ8.3.L5396Li
1994  [E]—dc20  93-26272  CIP  AC
ISBN: 0-671-88612-6

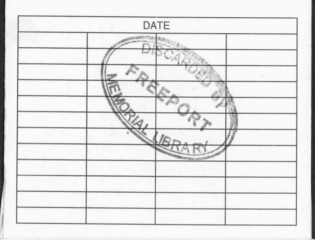